Haunted By Her

A SHORT, SMALL TOWN, MFF BISEXUAL, LOVE TRIANGLE ROMANCE

CORAL COVE
BOOK SEVEN

JAX WILDER

Published by Rainbow Quartz Publishing

RQPublishing.com

RainbowQuartzPublishing@gmail.com

Edmonds, WA 98026

This is a work of fiction. Names, characters, places, and incidents are either the product of the author's imagination or used fictitiously. Any resemblance to actual events, locales, or persons, living or dead, is entirely coincidental.

ISBN:978-1-961714-57-1

Cover design by Miranda Townsend

Edited by Miranda Townsend

First Edition: October, 2024

ONE

Molly

The brisk October wind swept through the streets of Coral Cove, tugging at the hem of my coat as I hurried towards the office. The town always felt different in the weeks leading up to Halloween—darker, more alive, as if it, too, held secrets beneath the surface. I pulled my scarf tighter against the wind's icy fingers, my thoughts drifting from the morning briefing to the small, locked drawer in my desk where I kept my secret. A secret that gnawed at me, especially in moments like this, when the veil between my worlds felt so thin I feared it might tear.

As I pushed through the front door of the Law Offices of Lorenzo Moretti, the familiar hum of the heater in the old building greeted me. I flipped on the lights, made my way to my desk, and grabbed a cup of coffee from the Keurig. It was the same ritual every year: pretend everything was normal, go about my day, and wait.

1

My husband, Ethan, had kissed me goodbye that morning, his lips warm against my cool cheek. "Don't forget, we still need to pick up the pumpkins tonight," he reminded me with a playful grin. He knew how much I loved Halloween, how I threw myself into the decorations, the costumes, and the thrill of it all. To him, it was just one of my quirks, one of the many reasons he loved me. But he didn't know the half of it.

As I sat at my desk, the drawer seemed to pulse with its own heartbeat, a steady thud that matched the one in my chest. I forced myself to focus on the tasks in front of me—shuffling papers, drafting emails—but the weight of the secret was always there, pressing down, stirring guilt within me.

I glanced at the photo of Ethan on my desk, his easy smile captured in a moment of pure joy. We were standing by a lake on a sunny afternoon, his arm wrapped around my shoulders, pulling me close, his love for me evident in his eyes. I traced a finger over the frame, my heart twisting. How much of me did he truly know? He knew when he married me that I was a liberal, spiritual, free-spirited bisexual woman. But the secret I kept hidden away in a locked drawer at my office was a lie he had no idea existed. That felt wrong.

The chime above the door startled me, and I nearly dropped my coffee cup. "Morning, Molly," Lorenzo's voice rang out, his usual warm greeting.

"Morning," I replied, forcing a smile that didn't quite reach my eyes.

"Didn't mean to startle you," he teased, grabbing his pile of mail from my desk. "Do you know if we got the court date for the Stewart case yet?"

"We did. I forwarded you the email from the clerk just a moment ago," I said.

"Perfect. Thank you, Molly," he replied before retreating to his office.

As soon as Lorenzo's door clicked shut, I exhaled slowly, the tightness in my chest easing a fraction. My hand drifted to the drawer, my fingers grazing the cool metal of the lock. It felt as though the drawer was calling to me, urging me to open it and touch the things that tethered me.

With a quick glance around to make sure I was alone, I slipped the small key from my pocket and turned it in the lock. The drawer slid open with a soft, almost inaudible creak. Inside, nestled beneath a pile of files, lay a small velvet pouch, its contents hidden but all too familiar to me. I lifted it gently, feeling the familiar weight of the objects within—the tools of ritual, the artifacts that were crucial.

My heart pounded in my ears as I loosened the drawstrings and peered inside. The faint scent of lavender and something more ancient drifted up, stirring memories I kept buried deep. My fingers brushed over the smooth surface of a polished stone, a delicate vial of shimmering liquid, and the scrap of paper with her handwriting, the words etched into my mind as clearly as if they were tattooed on my skin.

The spell—no, the ritual—had been carefully

crafted, its purpose singular and unavoidable. Every year, the same steps, the same incantations, the same longing that tugged at the corners of my heart.

I closed my eyes, the office fading away as the memories flooded back.

IT WAS DUSK. I STOOD IN SECLUDED SPOT DEEP IN THE woods, a place where trees grew thicker and the light barely penetrated the canopy. I had been drawn in years ago, the energy palpable in the air, buzzing against my skin. The small altar was already prepared, a simple arrangement of stones and herbs that seemed to vibrate with an otherworldly power.

Kneeling before the altar, I laid out the supplies just as I had been taught, each item placed with reverence. The words of the ritual spilled from my lips, soft at first, then gaining strength as the air around me seemed to hum in response.

And then she appeared, as she always did, her silhouette emerging from behind a towering oak. The first thing I noticed was the way the shadows seemed to cling to her, reluctant to let her go, reluctant to give her form. Her dress wasn't just black; it was the black of a moonless night, absorbing all light and leaving only an impression of where she stood. It moved like liquid, rippling with each step, whispering against the leaves as though it had secrets of its own.

Her eyes were the most unsettling part—not dark in color, but in depth. They were the color of old amber, rich and deep, yet within them was a darkness that seemed to swirl, like a storm brewing just beneath the surface.

When she looked at me, it was as though she could see right through to the part of me I kept hidden from everyone else, the part that only existed for her.

She crossed the distance between us with a grace that made my breath catch, her steps silent, predatory. When she reached me, she didn't speak. She never had to. Her hand cupped my cheek, her touch cool and electric, sending shivers down my spine. And then, without hesitation, her lips found mine, soft and insistent, stealing the breath from my lungs and the thoughts from my mind.

The kiss was intoxicating, a blend of hunger and tenderness that left me weak at the knees. I melted into her, the world spinning as her hands slipped around my waist, pulling me closer, grounding me even as she set me aflame.

I was hers, utterly and completely. In those moments, I was lost to the world, lost to Ethan, lost to everything but her.

THE MEMORY BURNED IN MY MIND AS I OPENED MY EYES, my fingers trembling slightly as I tightened the draw-strings of the velvet pouch and placed it back in the drawer. I closed it with a firm push, the lock clicking into place, but the weight of what I was hiding only grew heavier.

I took a deep breath, trying to steady myself and

focus on my job, but the ghost of her touch lingered on my lips. The guilt twisted in my gut like a living thing. Saturday night, I would see her again. And no matter how much I loved Ethan, no matter how perfect our life seemed, I knew I could never resist her call.

TWO

I stood in the middle of the living room, staring at the array of decorations scattered across the floor. Plastic pumpkins, strings of orange lights, and a cardboard skeleton grinned up at me as if mocking my uncertainty. Halloween had never been my favorite holiday. I much preferred the calm warmth of Thanksgiving or the magic of Christmas, but Molly had a way of pulling me into the spirit of things.

I knelt down and picked up a garland of fake autumn leaves, feeling the stiff plastic between my fingers. "Where the hell do these even go?" I muttered to myself, glancing around the room. It was already decorated enough, in my opinion, but Molly always liked going all out. If it made her happy, I would gladly dive into the chaos.

Starting with the garland, I draped it over the mantle above the fireplace, adjusting it until it looked somewhat natural. Stepping back, I put my hands on my hips and tilted my head. "Not bad," I said to the empty room, though I knew Molly would find a way to make it even better.

The doorbell rang, startling me out of my thoughts. I wiped my hands on my jeans as I walked over to the door, half-expecting to see a trick-or-treater who had gotten the dates mixed up. Instead, a delivery man stood on the porch, holding a large box decorated with pumpkins and bats.

"Ethan Parker?" the man asked.

"That's me," I replied, signing for the package and taking it inside. I set it down on the kitchen table and tore open the top. Inside, nestled among layers of tissue paper, were more decorations—this time, the really creepy ones that Molly loved. A pair of animatronic spiders that would probably send me jumping out of my skin if I didn't know they were fake, some cobweb material, and a set of black candles shaped like skulls. They bled red wax when lit.

I chuckled, shaking my head. "She's going to love these," I said to myself. As much as I didn't get the appeal of the spooky stuff, I couldn't help but admire Molly's enthusiasm. It was one of the things that had drawn me to her in the first place—her boundless energy and ability to make the mundane feel magical.

I sifted through the last crumpled sheets of tissue paper, my fingers brushing against something smooth and delicate at the bottom of the box. With a slight tug, I pulled out the final gift and unfolded it carefully in my hands.

It was a stunning black negligee, intricately designed with sheer, netted fabric resembling delicate spiderwebs woven together. The material shimmered faintly under the light, each thread catching the glow as if spun from midnight itself. As I held it up, the fabric cascaded down, draping elegantly and promising to cling to every curve, like a dark web that would envelop Molly in mystery and allure.

The front of my pants tighten just thinking about it. I reached down and adjusted myself, trying to make things a bit more comfortable. Clearly, this gift was more for me than for Molly, but I sensed she would love it nonetheless.

I got back to decorating, arranging the new items, hanging the cobwebs in the corners of the room, and placing the candles strategically around the house. The spiders I saved for last, dreading the moment they'd inevitably spring to life and scare the daylights out of me.

As I worked, my mind drifted to Molly. She'd been working late a lot recently, something about a big case that everyone at the firm was pulling extra hours for. I missed her, even though she made a point of sending me texts throughout the day. I loved the little reminders that she was thinking of me, too. We'd been married for five years now, and though the honeymoon phase was long over, there was still a deep warmth between us—a comfort in the way we understood each other without having to say much.

I set the last spider in place and looked around the living room. It was starting to feel more like Halloween, and even though it wasn't really my thing, I found myself smiling. Molly would be home soon, and the house would be ready for her.

I was just about to grab a soda from the fridge when I heard the jingle of keys at the front door. My heart lifted at the sound. I walked over to the entry-way, ready to greet her with a kiss.

When the door swung open and Molly stepped inside, my smile widened. "Hey, you," I said, taking in the sight of her. She was a little disheveled from the long day, but still beautiful in that effortless way she always managed.

"Wow," Molly said, looking around the room. "You really went all out."

I shrugged, trying to play it cool. "Just getting into the spirit."

Molly laughed, the sound filling the room with warmth. "I love it," she said, pulling me into a hug. I wrapped my arms around her, breathing in the scent of her perfume.

"I got you something else," I said with a sheepish grin, dancing over to the box on the couch and pulling out the bag containing the negligee.

"You didn't have to do that," she said, smiling. She carefully pulled out the negligee. "Oh my gods, this is stunning. Where did you find this?"

"Never mind that. Try it on quickly to make sure it fits," I suggested, starting to tug at her shirt, eager for the reveal.

Molly laughed and shook her head. "I'm going to put it on in the bedroom and then come out to do a reveal. This looks complicated to get on, and I don't want you to see the struggle."

I pretended to pout, but I couldn't help the grin that spread across my face. "Fine, I'll wait. But don't take too long."

Molly playfully swatted my arm as she headed towards the bedroom, holding the negligee carefully as if it were made of spun glass. I watched her go, anticipation buzzing in my chest. She paused at the doorway, throwing me a teasing glance over her shoulder. "Patience, mister. It'll be worth it."

"I'm counting on it," I called after her, already imagining how the delicate fabric would hug her body.

As the door clicked shut, I found myself pacing in the living room, my mind racing with thoughts of Molly in that stunning piece of lingerie. The image of her wrapped in those black webs made my pulse quicken. I could feel the tension in my body, the anticipation nearly unbearable.

A few minutes passed, each one dragging slower than the last. I busied myself by picking up Molly's coat and bags by the door. I put her coat away in the closet and emptied her bag onto the table. I grabbed her lunch box, pulling out the trash and rinsing it before setting it on the drying rack.

I reached for a small brown paper bag I didn't recognize. It had "Arcane Room" stamped on the outside. "Of course," I laughed. The Arcane Room was a mystical shop downtown, dangerously close to Molly's office, that carried all sorts of crystals and gemstones, herbs and incense, magical tools, books, and grimoires. I'd once joked with Ms. Vesper, the owner, that I might as well direct deposit her half of my paycheck every week.

Finally, I heard the soft click of the bedroom door opening, and I turned, my breath catching in my throat.

Molly stepped into the room, the light from the hallway casting a soft glow around her. The negligee clung to her in all the right places, the sheer fabric revealing just enough to leave little to the imagination while still maintaining an air of tantalizing mystery. The black spiderweb pattern wove across her skin, accentuating her curves and giving her an otherworldly allure that left me speechless.

She walked toward me with a shy smile, her cheeks flushed slightly as she did a slow twirl, letting the fabric dance around her legs. "So, what do you think?" she asked, her voice a mix of playfulness and uncertainty.

For a moment, I couldn't find the words. My mouth had gone dry, and all I could do was stare, completely captivated by her beauty. Finally, I managed to croak out, "You look… sexy as hell."

Molly's smile widened as she stepped closer, reaching out to take my hand. I led her in another spin to get a better view from behind.

"What do you think about it?" I asked.

She wrapped her arms around me, pulling me

close. I felt the cool, delicate fabric against my skin. "I think it's absolutely perfect. I feel like a sexy witch."

"A sexy witch, huh?"

"Don't you think?" she asked, making a playful claw-like gesture with her hand.

"I love it," I said. "And I love you."

She tilted her head up, her eyes meeting mine with a mischievous glint. "Why don't you show me just how much?"

My heart raced as I leaned in, capturing her lips in a deep, slow kiss. The warmth of her body pressed against mine, and the softness of the negligee heightened the sensation. The anticipation that had been building began to unravel, and I knew we were both about to lose ourselves in each other.

In one swift motion, I lifted my shirt off, pulling her close again. The contrast of her smooth, warm skin draped in the silky fabric against my bare chest made the pressure in my jeans unbearable. My hands instinctively moved down to the small of her back, savoring the curve of her waist before traveling lower to cup her perfect ass. I tugged gently at the fabric, hiking up the skirt portion of the negligee until her bare cheeks were exposed to my eager hands. The heat of her skin under my palms sent a shiver down my spine. I tightened my grip, lifting her slightly as I pressed her harder into the kiss, our mouths colliding with an intensity that left us both breathless.

Our tongues danced together, exploring and tasting, as I felt the weight of her body melt into mine.

She responded eagerly, her hands sliding up my back, nails grazing my skin and leaving a trail of tingling warmth in their wake. The soft fabric of the negligee brushed against my skin with every movement, heightening the sensation, making it feel like every nerve in my body was alive and on fire.

With a low growl, I lifted her higher, her legs automatically wrapping around my waist as I pressed her back against the wall. The pressure between us intensified, and I could feel the heat radiating from her as she moaned softly into my mouth—a sound that sent a surge of desire through me.

THREE

Molly

Breaking the kiss for a moment, Ethan looked into my eyes, dark and filled with the same hunger I felt, and whispered, "You're so damn beautiful."

My lips curled into a smile as his eyes stayed locked onto mine, the intensity between us growing. "Then show me," I said, and kissed him again.

Ethan needed no further invitation. He pulled me from the wall, my legs still wrapped around him, and carried me to the living room couch. He let me down with a thud, grabbing my thighs and pulling my hips over the edge of the seat. I could barely catch my breath before his face was at my center, kissing and teasing through the silky fabric.

I gasped and grabbed a handful of his hair as he worked, shaking his head quickly at my core. I stifled a giggle, letting out a moan to encourage him.

He pulled at the strings on either side of my panties, sliding the fabric aside to reveal my folds. He pressed his face against me, kissing and licking as if savoring every inch. Ethan trailed his tongue along my entrance, his movements gentle and exploratory.

I love this man, but he wasn't exactly skilled at oral. Still, I didn't want to discourage him, so when he asked, "You like that?" I replied with an enthusiastic, "Oh yeah. Now fuck me, baby."

Ethan stood up, unbuttoning his jeans. He quickly pulled them off, socks and all, leaving him standing in his tight red boxer briefs. The outline of his cock was evident, fully hard and eager. Thankfully, the gods blessed him with a well-endowed cock, and I couldn't help but admire the view.

He pulled off his boxers in one fluid motion, revealing his impressive length, hard and ready. I bit my lip, anticipation thrumming through my veins.

Ethan's eyes locked onto mine, dark with desire, as he positioned himself on his knees between my legs. The warmth of his body hovered just above mine, his erection grazing my inner thigh as he leaned in for another searing kiss. His hands roamed over my body, fingers exploring every curve, as if memorizing me.

Without breaking the kiss, Ethan reached down, guiding himself to my entrance. He paused, his breath hot against my neck, and I could feel the tension building.

"Ready?" he asked, his voice gritty with desire.

"More than ready," I breathed, wrapping my legs around his waist and pulling him closer, urging him on.

With a slow, deliberate thrust, Ethan entered me, filling me completely. The sensation was intense, a mix of pleasure and pressure that made me gasp. He began to move, his rhythm steady but deep, each stroke sending waves of heat coursing through me. I arched my back, meeting him with every thrust, the friction building with each movement.

Ethan's hands gripped my hips, pulling me closer as he picked up the pace, his breath ragged against my ear. I could feel the muscles in his back tense under my fingers, every movement perfectly synchronized with mine, driving us both closer to the edge.

"Gods, you feel so good," he groaned, his voice raw with need.

The intensity of his thrusts increased, and I felt the coil of pleasure tightening deep within me. I reached out, grabbing a handful of his chest hair, my nails digging into his skin as I held on, riding the wave of sensation that threatened to consume me.

"Ethan… I'm so close," I whispered, my voice barely audible over the sounds of our bodies moving together.

"Me too," he panted, his rhythm faltering as he neared his own release.

With one final, powerful thrust, he pushed us both over the edge. I cried out as the orgasm washed over me, every nerve alight with pleasure. Ethan followed moments later, his body tensing as he emptied himself inside me, his groan low and primal.

For a moment, we were both still, breathing

heavily as the aftershocks of our release rippled through us. Then Ethan collapsed beside me, our backs resting on the couch, our legs tangled and our lower halves hanging awkwardly over the edge. We lay there, bodies slick with sweat and heat.

"I love you," he murmured against my hair, his voice soft as the passion of the moment gave way to tenderness.

"I love you too," I whispered back, snuggling into his embrace, feeling content and blissfully satiated. I was perfectly happy right there, wrapped in the warmth of Ethan, the scent of our lovemaking lingering in the air.

Yet, even as I basked in the afterglow, thoughts of the witch slipped into my mind. I tried to shake them off, focusing on the man beside me, the man I loved. But the excitement, the anticipation of seeing her on Halloween night, was like an itch I couldn't scratch. It lingered at the back of my mind, a tantalizing thrill that I couldn't ignore.

I shook my head slightly, hoping to dislodge thoughts of her. I couldn't let her overshadow this moment, not when I was so happy with Ethan. But she had a way of seeping into my thoughts, especially as the day drew nearer.

With a sigh, I gently disentangled myself from Ethan's embrace and stood up, feeling the cool air against my skin. He looked up at me with a lazy, satisfied smile. "Where are you going?"

"I'm just going to change into something more comfortable," I replied, returning his smile. "And maybe start messing around with the Halloween decorations."

Ethan chuckled, his eyes half-closed with post-ejaculatory drowsiness. "That's my girl. You're insatiable when it comes to Halloween."

I smiled and made my way to the bathroom, carefully slipping out of the negligee and inspecting it for any staining before draping it on a hanger.

After freshening up, I went to the bedroom and pulled on a pair of soft leggings and an oversized sweatshirt—the kind of clothes that made me feel cozy and relaxed.

When I returned to the living room, Ethan had stretched out fully on the couch, still completely naked. He looked entirely too comfortable for someone who had just been thoroughly ravished. I smiled at the sight of him, a rush of affection warming my chest. He really was everything I could ask for in a husband. I walked over and lightly grabbed at the tip of his dick.

"Hey!" he shouted, curling up to protect himself. "You know you can't do that to me." He grinned, covering himself with his hands.

Ethan was incredibly sensitive after sex. Early on, I'd tried to go down on him after he came, and he'd jerked back so hard he'd hit the wall. Now I knew better. Even the slightest touch made him recoil, although it never hurt him, and it always made me laugh.

He gave me a playful slap on the butt as payback.

I turned my attention to the box of decorations

that still needed unpacking. Ethan had made a good start, but I wanted more. I liked our house to look like an abandoned witch's cottage in the woods for the week of Halloween.

The task kept my hands busy, but my mind couldn't help but wander. As I adjusted a particularly stubborn garland, I glanced at Ethan, who had dozed off, his chest rising and falling in a steady rhythm. Thoughts of the witch returned, unbidden. Her dark presence, her velvety skin, the way she made me feel alive and reckless.

I felt a pang of guilt for thinking about her while Ethan slept nearby, so content and happy. But I couldn't deny the flutter of excitement at the thought of Halloween night.

I shook my head, focusing on the task at hand. For now, I would enjoy this quiet evening with Ethan, making our home ready for the holiday. The witch would come soon enough, and I'd deal with those feelings when the time came.

FOUR

Ethan

I had no idea how long I'd been asleep on the couch, but when I finally stirred, I noticed that Molly had been sweet enough to cover me with a blanket. The soft fabric was draped over my bare body, a small but thoughtful gesture that brought a smile to my face.

I blinked a few times, trying to shake off the remnants of sleep, and looked around for her. The living room was quiet, and Molly was nowhere to be seen. A slight unease crept into my chest as I sat up, the blanket slipping off my shoulders.

My mind drifted back to the passionate moments we'd just shared. Our lovemaking had been intense, as always, but there was something I couldn't quite put my finger on. Something about Molly felt... off. It wasn't anything obvious, nothing I could easily describe, but it lingered at the back of my mind, gnawing at me.

Maybe it was the way she'd looked at me afterward, a little too distant, as if she were a thousand miles away even while wrapped in my arms. Or maybe it was just the weight of everything—her work, the holidays, and all the little stresses that had been piling up lately. I shook my head, trying to dismiss the thought. I was probably overthinking things. Molly had been working long hours, and we'd been caught up in the whirlwind of preparing for Halloween. It was natural to feel a little off-balance.

Still, the feeling nagged at me as I stood up, stretching out the stiffness in my muscles. I reached for my clothes, which were haphazardly tossed on the floor, and dressed. The house felt too quiet without her, and I felt an urge to find her, make sure everything was okay. I reminded myself: she gets weird every Halloween.

After pulling on my t-shirt, I padded around the living room, half-expecting to find her in the kitchen or maybe fiddling with the decorations I hadn't quite finished. But as I turned the corner into the hallway, I noticed a small note taped to the fridge. I plucked it off and read it:

Went to grab Halloween candy. Be back soon!

I smiled, though the unease in my chest didn't fully dissipate. I picked up my phone and dialed her number, listening to the ring as I walked to the front window and looked out at the street.

"Hey," Molly's voice came through the line, her softness always managing to calm me, even when my thoughts were running wild.

"Hey," I replied. "I got your note. Thought I'd catch up with you. Where are you?"

"Just made it to the store," she said, and I could hear the hum of the town in the background. "Why? Miss me already?"

I chuckled. "Always. How about I meet you at the pumpkin patch? We were planning to carve them tomorrow."

"Sounds good," she agreed, her voice lightening. "I'll see you there in a bit."

We hung up, and I grabbed my keys from the hook by the door, shrugging on a jacket as I headed out. The crisp autumn air greeted me as I stepped into the driveway, a welcome contrast to the warmth that still clung to me from our time on the couch.

As I made my way through town, I spotted a familiar Toyota up ahead. "Good timing," I muttered to myself. I picked up speed to get right behind her. I could see the top of her head barely peeking out above the seat.

She made a left onto Water Street.

"That's not the way to the pumpkin patch," I said, deciding to follow. I turned left behind her.

Molly continued down Water Street. She could, in theory, turn at the end and loop back around, but that would add several miles to the trip. Maybe she forgot something at the office? We passed by her office.

Nope.

She pulled into a parking spot a few blocks down.

I continued past her and then pulled into a spot eight or nine spaces to the east.

I watched as Molly stepped out of the car and made her way into Spellbound Stories Bookstore. The shop was one of those eclectic little places that smelled of old paper and incense, with shelves stacked high with books on everything from world history and folklore to the occult. It was one of Molly's favorite haunts, but she hadn't mentioned anything about needing to stop by today.

Curiosity piqued, I decided to surprise her and slipped out of my car, crossing the street and into the shop. I pushed open the door as gently as I could, the bell tinkling softly above me. The cozy interior was dimly lit, with narrow aisles winding between towering bookshelves. I spotted Molly near the counter, talking to Lea, the shop's owner—a spunky, curvy thirty-something with a loud mane of orange hair.

I moved closer, staying just out of sight behind a shelf filled with old leather-bound grimoires. Molly leaned in slightly, speaking in a hushed tone, though the shop was empty except for the three of us.

"I'm here to pick up the order of sulfur powder," Molly said, her voice low and serious. I couldn't help but scrunch up my face. *Sulfur powder?* That was unusual.

Lea nodded, reaching under the counter and pulling out a small brown paper bag. "I've got it right here," she said, her tone casual. "Ms. Vesper called; you should have everything you need now."

Molly accepted the bag, slipping it into her purse, then fished out her wallet to pay. I stayed rooted to the spot, unsure of what to make of the exchange. *What could she possibly need sulfur powder for?* My mind raced, trying to come up with a plausible explanation, but nothing made sense.

As Lea rang her up, I took a deep breath and stepped out from behind the shelf, just in time to see Molly finish her transaction. She turned to leave, her purse slung over her shoulder, and nearly collided with me.

"Ethan!" she gasped, her eyes wide with surprise. Her hand flew to her chest as she caught her breath. "What are you doing here?"

I raised an eyebrow, trying to keep my tone light even though my mind was buzzing with questions. "I could ask you the same thing. I was on my way to the pumpkin patch and saw you. I followed you here. I'm surprised you didn't see me behind you."

Molly blinked, clearly caught off guard. "I... I was just picking up a few things. I forgot I needed to stop by the bookstore."

"For sulfur powder?" I asked, unable to keep the curiosity out of my voice. I wasn't accusing her of anything, but I couldn't ignore the oddity of the situation.

Her eyes flickered with something I couldn't quite read. Nervousness, maybe? She quickly masked it with a smile. "Oh, that. It's for a little project I'm working on for Halloween."

I wanted to believe her, and maybe I was overreacting, but I couldn't shake the feeling that something more was going on. Now wasn't the time to press her on it, though.

I forced a smile and nodded. "Okay, just make sure you keep that stuff in the garage. It stinks."

She laughed, the sound a bit too forced for my liking, but it eased the tension. "I promise."

"Alright," I said, stepping back to give her some space. "Ready to head to the pumpkin patch?"

Molly nodded, her smile genuine this time. "Yeah, let's go."

As we left the shop together, I glanced back at Lea, who was watching us with a strange expression on her face. There was something unsettling about the whole encounter, but I pushed it aside. Molly was my wife, and I trusted her. Whatever she was up to was probably for some quirky Halloween project she'd seen on Pinterest.

Later at the pumpkin patch, as we walked hand in hand in the crisp autumn air, I couldn't completely shake the unease that had settled in the pit of my stomach. Whatever Molly was planning, I just hoped it wouldn't come back to haunt us.

FIVE

Molly

The scent of hay and earth mixed with the faint aroma of hot apple cider wafting from a nearby stand as we made our way through the pumpkin patch. Families and couples meandered between rows of pumpkins, their laughter and chatter a distant hum. But between Ethan and me, there was a silence that felt heavier than the largest pumpkin in the field.

I glanced at him from the corner of my eye. He seemed absorbed in the task of finding the perfect pumpkins, his brow furrowed slightly as he examined one that was particularly lopsided. But I could tell his mind was elsewhere, probably still stuck on what he saw back at the bookstore.

The sulfur powder.

One of the necessary ingredients I needed for my ritual on Saturday. I mentally kicked myself for not coming up with a better excuse when he caught me off guard. The truth was, I hadn't expected him to follow me into Spellbound Books, and when he showed up behind me, my mind went blank. Now, the awkwardness between us was palpable, and I was sure he felt it too. If I'm being honest, I was slightly relieved—maybe it was time to tell him.

"Hey, what do you think about this one?" Ethan's voice broke through my thoughts. He held up a medium-sized pumpkin, its surface a smooth, deep orange.

"It's nice," I replied, forcing a smile that felt a little too tight on my face. "Perfect for carving."

He nodded, placing the pumpkin in the wagon we had borrowed from the patch's entrance. But instead of moving on, he hesitated, his gaze lingering on me longer than usual. I could see the questions in his eyes, the ones he hadn't asked yet, simmering just beneath the surface.

I pretended not to notice, crouching down to inspect a smaller pumpkin, running my fingers over its cool, bumpy skin. The silence stretched between us again, more strained this time. I knew I should say something, anything, to break the tension, but my words caught in my throat.

Ethan cleared his throat, shifting on his feet. He opened his mouth to say something but stopped.

I straightened up to meet his gaze, and for a moment, I considered telling him everything. But the words didn't come. Instead, I returned to the pumpkins. "What about this one?"

"I think it's a little too bumpy for carving. I mean,

depends on what you want to do, I guess," he replied.

"Yeah, I thought this bumpy section could work for a witch's face, but I think you're right—it's easier to start with a flat surface," I said, offering a smile.

Ethan nodded slowly, but I could tell he wasn't entirely present. His eyes searched mine, and I had to resist the urge to look away. I hated lying to him, but how could I explain the real reason without opening a door I wasn't ready for him to walk through?

"Ethan," I said quietly.

"Yes?"

"I love you," I said without a smile.

"Okay," Ethan replied, stepping closer and wrapping an arm around me.

I leaned into him, pulling my sweater tighter around myself against the crisp autumn air. I breathed him in, catching the scent of sex mixed with his natural, masculine aroma.

"I kind of thought there was going to be a 'but' after that 'I love you,'" Ethan added a beat later.

"No but. I love you," I said.

"Aww, I love you too, Molly," he replied, leaning in to kiss the top of my head.

I smiled up at him, but it didn't quite reach his eyes. We continued walking through the patch, but the easy, lighthearted vibe that usually accompanied our trips to pick out pumpkins was gone. Instead, an awkward tension clung to the air between us, growing heavier with each step.

And it was all my fault.

I picked out another pumpkin, handing it to Ethan without meeting his eyes, and we continued this uncomfortable dance—both of us aware, but neither willing to confront it head-on.

Near the exit of the pumpkin patch, they had a beautiful fall display, something an artist developed every year. It was our tradition to take a picture there —a snapshot of each autumn we'd spent together, documenting the years in a growing series of photos that lined the hallway of our home. This year's theme was an unusual blend of Halloween and Valentine's Day. It was a mix of hay bales, cornstalks, and gigantic sunflowers adorned with bright red roses, green garlands, and delicate sprigs of baby's breath. It was an odd combination, but somehow it worked.

Ethan stopped and turned to me, a soft smile playing on his lips. "Ready for our annual picture?" he asked, the tension in his voice easing as he gestured toward the photographer.

I looked at the scene, the vibrant colors contrasting sharply against the earth tones of the season, and felt a twinge of guilt in my chest. This was our tradition, a moment we always cherished, but the thought of capturing this memory this year, with this awkward tension, made my stomach churn.

I forced a smile and nodded. "Sure, let's take the picture," I said, trying to ignore the knot tightening in my stomach. Ethan's face lit up with relief, his smile widening as he reached for my hand and guided me toward the display.

We stood in front of the setup, the photographer

giving us a cheerful wave as he adjusted his camera. I felt the familiar weight of tradition settling over us, but instead of comfort, it felt like a chain tightening around my chest. The roses and baby's breath entwined with the pumpkins and cornstalks were meant to symbolize a blend of love and the season's change, but all I could think about was Saturday night, when I would be with the witch.

Ethan wrapped his arm around my waist, pulling me close as we faced the camera. I tried to steady my breath, to focus on the moment, but the thought of taking this picture, capturing this memory, felt like a betrayal I couldn't shake.

The photographer lifted his camera, his finger hovering over the shutter button. "Alright, you two, say cheese!"

Just as he was about to snap the photo, a surge of panic rose in my chest. I couldn't do it—I couldn't pretend everything was fine. Without thinking, I turned to Ethan, grabbing his hand and pulling him away from the display.

"Molly, what…" Ethan began, confusion in his voice, but I didn't let him finish. I led him away from the photographer, from the scene that felt like it was mocking me, until we were out of earshot, near a quiet row of pumpkins.

Ethan looked at me, concern etched into his features. "What's going on?" he asked, his voice low, the earlier confusion now replaced with worry.

I took a deep breath, trying to calm the storm inside of me. "Ethan, I'm sorry," I began, my voice trembling. "I thought I could go through with it, but I just… can't."

He frowned, his grip on my hand tightening slightly. "Can't what? Take the picture?"

"No," I said, shaking my head. "It's not the picture. It's… everything. There's something I need to tell you, something I should have told you a long time ago."

Ethan's face grew more serious, his brow furrowing. "Molly, you're scaring me. What's going on?"

"I haven't been completely honest with you," I confessed, my heart racing. "Every year, on Halloween night… there's someone else. But it's not what you think. It's not a normal affair."

His hand dropped from mine as the words hit him. His face went pale. "What the hell are you talking about? Someone else?" His voice wavered between disbelief and hurt.

"It's a witch, Ethan," I said, forcing the words out. "I know it sounds crazy, but she's real. Every year on All Hallows' Eve, she comes to me, and I can't resist her. It's like I'm under her spell."

For a moment, Ethan just stared at me, like he couldn't comprehend what I was saying. Then he shook his head, taking a step back. "A witch? Molly, this doesn't make any sense." His voice rose, disbelief edging into anger now. "You're telling me you've been having an affair with—what, some kind of supernatural being? And you kept this from me?"

I could see the hurt in his eyes, a deep, growing pain. I tried to reach for him, but he stepped back again, his arms folding across his chest. "I didn't want to hurt you, Ethan. I'm telling you now because I can't keep hiding this. It's more than just... cheating. It's something else entirely."

His face hardened. "Cheating is cheating, Molly. Whether it's with a person or a damn witch!" His voice cracked slightly, the raw hurt bubbling to the surface. "How long has this been going on? How long have you been lying to me?"

I swallowed, my throat dry. "Years. Since before we got married."

Ethan looked like he'd been slapped. He ran a hand through his hair, his chest rising and falling with quick breaths as he tried to make sense of it. "You've been doing this behind my back for years? Jesus, Molly. What the hell am I supposed to do with that?"

Tears welled up in my eyes. "I didn't know how to tell you... I was scared of what it would mean."

"Scared of what it would mean?" he repeated, incredulous. "You didn't think it might mean you were betraying me?" His words cut deep, and I could see the pain in his eyes, raw and open. "You... you said you loved me. We built a life together, Molly. And now you're telling me you've been in love with someone else this whole time?"

"I do love you," I whispered, my voice shaking. "You give me everything—a love that's stable, real, something I couldn't live without. You're my best friend, my partner."

Ethan's jaw clenched, his eyes hardening as he

fought to hold back his emotions. "But that wasn't enough for you. You needed more." It wasn't a question. It was a bitter realization.

"I needed something different," I admitted, my voice breaking. "With her, it's… it's like I'm tapping into something darker, something I can't find anywhere else. It's not just desire—it's something deeper. She gives me a sense of power, of freedom."

Ethan let out a bitter laugh, rubbing his hands over his face. "So that's it? You're in love with both of us? You get something from her that I can't give you?"

"I don't know," I whispered. "I don't have all the answers. All I know is that I love you both, in different ways. And I didn't want to hurt you, but I can't deny what I feel for her."

Ethan stared at me, his face a mix of devastation and anger. "You lied to me for years, Molly. How am I supposed to just… be okay with that?"

"I don't expect you to be okay with it," I said, the tears flowing freely now. "I'm telling you because I can't keep lying. I want to figure this out with you. I don't want to lose you."

He turned away, his shoulders tense, his hands clenched into fists at his sides. "I can't… I can't even look at you right now." His voice was low, broken. "I need some space."

I reached out again, but he stepped further away, his back turned to me. "Ethan, please—"

"I need time, Molly," he said, his voice hard.

"Time to figure out what the hell I'm supposed to do with this. With us."

The weight of his words sank deep into my chest, a sinking, suffocating feeling. I watched him walk away, the distance between us growing not just physically, but emotionally—an endless chasm that might never be bridged.

SIX

I was relieved, in a strange way, that Molly had finally told me what was going on with her. I'd been bracing myself for something entirely different—an affair with another man, a gut punch that would have left me reeling. But when she confessed her love for a witch, my mind struggled to process it.

A witch? Was that even real?

And if it was real, was that even technically cheating? It felt surreal, like something out of a story, not something that could actually happen in real life. Yet, here we were.

My thoughts churned as I tried to make sense of it. If she'd told me she was seeing another man, it would've been simpler, in a way. It would have hurt like hell, but it was something I could understand. It would have fit within the boundaries of what people typically go through. But this... this was different.

This was something I hadn't ever imagined dealing with.

I found myself grappling with what she even meant by "witch." Was this some kind of metaphor? Or was she serious? And then a thought struck me— Calliope Vesper. No one ever called her anything but Ms. Vesper, yet Molly had always been on a first-name basis with her. I couldn't help but wonder if Molly was talking about *her*. Calliope was more than a little strange, always surrounded by mystery, and there were plenty of rumors about her and that *Arcane Room* of hers. Could it be her? Had Molly been involved with Calliope this whole time?

I shook my head, trying to focus. I'd always worried, deep down, that I wouldn't be able to give Molly everything she needed. I knew she was bisexual, and while that never bothered me, there was always a small, nagging fear that I wouldn't be enough for her. That she'd want something more, something I couldn't provide. Maybe this was part of that fear coming to life, but in a way I never expected.

Yet, despite how bizarre it all was, there was also a strange sense of relief. She hadn't lied about another man. Instead, this was... well, something entirely different. A witch. A woman. And somehow, that felt like something I could at least try to understand.

"Are you okay?" Molly's voice broke through my thoughts, pulling me back to the present. I'm not sure how long she had been standing there.

"I'm still just processing," I admitted honestly. "I have a lot of questions."

"I'd honestly be surprised if you didn't," she replied, her eyes watching me closely.

I wasn't sure how to feel about it all yet, but I knew one thing: I wasn't going to let this destroy us. I loved Molly, and if she needed this—if this was part of who she was—I was going to find a way to make peace with it. Because I loved her, and I'd do whatever it took to make our relationship work, even if it meant navigating this strange new reality.

I took a deep breath, feeling the weight of the situation settle on my shoulders. "We'll have to have a much longer conversation about this later," I said, my voice steady. "But for now, I want you to know that I love you. Nothing you've told me changes that. I love every part of you, Molly, even the parts that are complicated and messy. You are my everything, and we're going to figure this out together."

Molly's eyes shimmered with emotion, and she let out a deep breath. "I love you too, Ethan. So much."

I reached out, brushing a stray strand of hair from her face, my thumb gently caressing her cheek. "You've always been honest with me about who you are, and that's one of the things I love most about you. This might be new and unexpected, but it's part of you, and I'm here for all of it."

Her lips curled into a soft, relieved smile, and she leaned into my touch, closing her eyes for a moment as if soaking in my words. "Thank you," she whispered, her voice thick with emotion. "I didn't know how you'd react, but... this means everything to me."

I pulled her into a gentle embrace, holding her close. "You mean everything to me, Molly. We'll take this one step at a time, together."

She nodded against my chest, her arms tightening around me. For a moment, we stood there, wrapped in each other, letting the world around us fade away. I could feel the tension between us melting, replaced by a renewed sense of connection.

After a few moments, I pulled back slightly, tilting her chin up so I could look into her eyes. "How about we go take that picture now?" I suggested, my tone light.

Molly smiled, this time a genuine, radiant smile that reached her eyes. "I'd like that."

We walked back to the display, hand in hand, and stood in front of the setup once more. The photographer gave us a curious glance, as if sensing the shift in our energy, but said nothing as he lifted his camera again.

"Alright," the photographer said, his voice cheerful. "Let's try this one more time. Big smiles!"

I wrapped my arm around Molly's waist, pulling her close as we both smiled for the camera. The flash went off, capturing the moment in a burst of light.

After, I glanced at the screen on the photographer's camera as he showed us the shot. My breath caught when I saw Molly's smile—genuine, bright, and full of happiness. It was the kind of smile that lit up her whole face, the kind that made my heart swell with love.

In that moment, I knew we were going to be okay. We were a team, and this was just another part of our journey.

I looked at Molly, and she looked back at me, her eyes shining with love and gratitude. "Thank you, Ethan," she whispered, squeezing my hand.

I smiled, leaning down to press a soft kiss to her forehead. "Always," I whispered back.

We paid for the photo and the pumpkins, and soon after, we were heading to our car, the photo in hand.

When we arrived home, we unloaded the pumpkins and hung this year's photo next to the others in the hallway. It felt right, like adding another chapter to our story. We collapsed once again on the couch in the living room.

I sat there, still trying to process everything. My mind circled back to one specific question that had been nagging at me ever since she'd said the word "witch."

"Molly, is it… is it Calliope Vesper?" I asked, my voice tinged with uncertainty. "You're always on a first-name basis with her, and nobody else calls her that. Is she the witch you're talking about?"

Molly's eyes widened in surprise before she quickly shook her head. "No, no—it's not Ms. Vesper," she said, her voice firm but soft. "I mean, she's strange, sure, and the Arcane Room rumors don't help, but no. Elizabeth isn't her."

A wave of relief washed over me, though I still felt unsettled. "So, when did you meet this Elizabeth?"

Molly hesitated for a moment, her fingers nervously fiddling with the edge of her sleeve. "It's been six years now," she admitted, her voice quieter. "I met her the same year I met you."

I blinked, the weight of her words settling over me. "Six years," I repeated, trying to wrap my head around it. "So… you met her around the same time you met me?"

She nodded, her gaze shifting to the floor. "Yeah. It didn't seem like it mattered at first. I thought it was all a dream, honestly. After that first night, I wasn't sure if it had really happened. I didn't think it was real… but I had to follow through the second year to be sure."

"And that's when you realized it wasn't just some dream?"

Molly nodded again. "We talked all night that second year. And that was the first time I was… sexually intimate with a woman. I'd kissed a few girls before, but Elizabeth was the first—and the only—woman I've been with."

I could hear the vulnerability in her voice, the weight of what she was confessing. I stayed quiet, letting her continue.

"At first, it felt like this fun secret, like something

separate from the rest of my life," she said, her voice trembling slightly. "But then… then you and I got engaged so fast. I went to see her the third year, planning to end it. I wanted to tell her that it couldn't continue, that I loved you, and I didn't want to risk what we had."

I could feel a lump forming in my throat as I listened to her. "What happened?"

Molly's lips twisted into a sad smile. "I couldn't do it. I love her, Ethan. I tried to tell her goodbye, but I couldn't bring myself to walk away. I told her all about you, about us. About how happy I am with you. I told her I didn't want to risk what we have."

She paused, her voice growing softer. "Elizabeth encouraged me to tell you. She told me right there— call you, have you come meet us. But I was scared. I was so afraid of losing you, of ruining everything by keeping this secret. But I can't keep lying anymore. I want you to know all of me, and Elizabeth… she's part of that."

I let out a slow breath, absorbing everything she was telling me. Six years. For six years, she had been carrying this other relationship alongside ours. Part of me felt the weight of betrayal, but another part of me—maybe the bigger part—just wanted to understand. To make sense of it all.

"So, when do I get to meet this witch?" I asked, breaking the silence, my voice calm but filled with curiosity.

Molly's body tensed slightly. "Oh," she responded, startled by the question.

"I mean, I feel like I have to meet her," I said, my tone calm but firm. "If she's going to be a part of our lives, I need to understand it. I need to see her."

Molly shifted, sitting up slightly to face me. "Well, yeah... that makes sense, of course," she admitted, her eyes searching mine for understanding. "But she's only around for one night a year—on Halloween."

I nodded, encouraging her to continue. "Okay, so how does it work? What do I need to know?"

She took a deep breath, as if gathering her thoughts. "It's complicated," she began, her voice soft. "There's a ritual I perform every year at an altar in the middle of the woods. I've been doing it for years now. It's an ancient spell that brings her back from the beyond, just for that one night."

I listened intently as she explained, describing the steps of the ritual, the way she prepared the altar with candles and offerings, the words of the spell she recited to summon Elizabeth. There was a reverence in her voice as she spoke, a deep connection to the magic she wielded. I could tell this was more than just a ritual for her. It was something sacred, something that had become a part of who she was.

"And then she appears," Molly continued, her eyes distant as she recalled the moment. "It's like she steps out of the shadows, fully formed, as if she's always been there. We spend the night together. It's intense, Ethan. It's like nothing else."

I absorbed her words, trying to wrap my head around the reality of it. It was surreal, yes, but I could see how much it meant to her, how important this connection with Elizabeth was. And despite the strangeness of it all, I couldn't deny the feeling that was growing within me—a deep desire to understand and fully be a part of this aspect of her life.

"Okay, can I come for the ritual and meet her?" I asked, my voice steady. "I feel like I need to see this to believe it all."

Molly looked at me, her eyes a mixture of surprise and relief. "You really want to be there? For the ritual?"

I nodded. "If this is important to you, then it's important to me. I want to be there and see this part of your life."

She smiled, a hint of uncertainty in her eyes, but mostly gratitude. "Okay, I'll make sure you're there. It might be... strange, but if you're sure..."

"I'm sure," I said, cutting her off gently. "I need to see this. I want to understand what it means to you, and if that means I take off after she appears, then that's what I'll do."

Molly's smile grew, the tension between us easing as she leaned in, pressing her lips to mine in a soft, tender kiss. "Thank you, Ethan. It means more to me than you know."

I wrapped my arms around her, pulling her close again. "I never want you to feel like you have to hide anything from me. Even if it's something scary, we'll face it together, okay?"

"Absolutely," she said.

We sat there in silence for a while, the fire crackling softly beside us. There was still so much to process, so many questions left unanswered, but for now, we were together, and that was enough.

And come this Saturday, on Halloween night, I would meet Elizabeth—the other piece of Molly's heart.

SEVEN
Molly

We laid there on the floor of the living room, in front of the fireplace, my head resting gently on Ethan's chest. I looked up at the man I married with such awe and adoration. He really saw me for who I was—every complicated piece of me—and still loved me with his whole heart. It was a love that made me feel safe, cherished, and understood in a way I never thought possible.

I reached up, tracing the line of his jaw with my fingertips, feeling the warmth of his skin beneath my touch. "You're an incredible man, Ethan," I whispered, my voice filled with emotion. "I don't think I tell you that enough."

He smiled down at me, his eyes soft and full of affection. "I just want you to be happy, Molly. That's all I've ever wanted."

A surge of love for him welled up inside me, so

powerful it made my chest ache. I lifted myself slightly, pressing my lips to his in a tender kiss, pouring all my gratitude and affection into that simple gesture. He responded, his hand sliding into my hair, pulling me closer.

But tonight, I wanted to show him how much he meant to me, how much I appreciated his understanding, patience, and love. I wanted to give back to him, to make him feel the same pleasure and contentment he always gave me.

I broke the kiss, looking into his eyes with a soft smile. "I want to do something for you," I said, my voice gentle but firm.

He raised an eyebrow, his smile turning playful. "And what would that be?"

"Just let me take care of you tonight," I replied, my head resting on his chest, feeling the steady beat of his heart beneath my palm. "You've done so much for me, and I want to make you feel good. Just sit back and enjoy it. Let me do this for you."

Ethan looked at me for a moment, as if weighing his desire to participate against the sincerity in my voice. Finally, he nodded, a soft chuckle escaping his lips. "Alright," he said, his voice low and full of warmth. "I'll do whatever you want."

I smiled and kissed him again, but this time with more intensity, more passion. My hands began to explore his body, massaging the tension from his shoulders, down his arms, and across his chest. I could feel him relax beneath my touch, his muscles loosening as I worked, my fingers kneading away the stress of the day.

I kissed along his neck, feeling the pulse beneath his skin, and continued down his chest, trailing my lips over every inch of him. My hands moved lower, finding all the spots that made him sigh in pleasure. It wasn't just about the physical pleasure; I wanted to show him how much I valued him, how deeply I loved him.

Ethan's breaths grew heavier. "Molly... you're amazing," he mumbled.

"Just relax," I whispered against his skin, my hands continuing their journey. "Let me take care of you."

He closed his eyes, surrendering to my touch, letting me guide him through this moment.

Tonight was about us—about our love—and I was determined to make him feel as cherished and adored as he made me feel every single day.

I pulled his t-shirt up, exposing his stomach, and gently kissed my way up his chest, pulling the shirt ahead of my kisses. He lifted his back slightly to help me remove the shirt completely before resting back down, all the while keeping his eyes shut tight.

I gently massaged his nipples between my index finger and thumb. He let out labored breaths, squirming underneath me. I ran my fingernails through his chest hair, pulling gently at several spots across his chest.

My tongue traced slow, deliberate circles down

his chest, each soft kiss a promise of more to come. I could feel his heartbeat quickening beneath my lips, a steady rhythm that echoed the rising tension between us. His breaths came in short, uneven gasps as I continued, savoring him, watching carefully how he responded to every touch.

As I reached the center of his chest, I paused, letting my fingers trail lightly over his skin, feeling the way his muscles tensed and relaxed under my touch. I could sense his growing anticipation, the way his body instinctively leaned into my caresses, craving more yet content to let me set the pace.

I leaned in closer, my lips hovering above his skin, letting my warm breath wash over him. I could feel the slight tremble in his body, the way his chest rose and fell. He kept his eyes shut tight, surrendering completely to the sensations, trusting me to lead him through this moment.

Gently, I moved lower, kissing along the line of his ribs. I could feel the heat radiating from his skin, the subtle shift of his muscles as he squirmed beneath me.

I let my fingers dance across his abdomen, my touch light and teasing, tracing the contours of his body.

My lips followed the path of my fingers, kissing lower just above the waistband of his sweatpants. I could see the tension in him, the way his body seemed to hum with energy, ready to burst but held in check by the fabric of his clothes.

I paused there, taking a moment to look up at him, to see the way his lips parted in quiet surrender, his eyes still closed, completely lost in the sensations. It was a beautiful sight, knowing that I was the one bringing him to this place of pure bliss.

I let my hands roam up and down his sides, feeling the contrast between the firm muscle beneath and the softness of his skin. Each touch was intentional, meant to heighten his awareness and draw out pleasure in a delicate way.

As I continued to explore his body, my touch growing more assured. But instead of rushing, I maintained my slow, deliberate pace, savoring each moment, each small reaction from him. This wasn't about raw, urgent need; it was about connection and showing him how deeply I adored and cherished every part of him.

I pressed another kiss below his navel, my hands gently kneading his hips, my fingers brushing the sensitive skin just above his sweatpants. He let out a soft moan, his body shuddering under my touch, and I smiled against his skin, knowing this was only the beginning.

He started to reach for me, but I gently placed my hand on his, guiding it back down to his side. He let out a deep sigh, his body relaxing back into the floor, his hands falling away as he surrendered. His trust in me, the way he let me lead, made my heart swell with affection.

I kissed lower, letting my hands wander freely, touching and caressing, bringing him closer and closer to the edge but always holding back just enough to keep him in that sweet, torturous state of anticipation. I kissed the space to the left of his center, letting my cheek brush against his swollen member. I could feel it pulse against my skin, but I moved back up to his navel.

My fingers danced around the front of his sweatpants, making gentle, teasing strokes over his bulge. He quivered beneath my touch, his breath hitching as I applied just enough pressure to keep him on edge.

I slipped my fingers under his waistband and pulled down his pants and boxer briefs in one swoop. His cock sprang free with a quick thwap against his stomach.

Ethan cried out in surprise.

"Oh, I'm sorry, babe," I said, feeling terrible.

"It's okay," Ethan said with an exhale.

"Should I kiss it and make it all better?" I asked with a mischievous grin.

"Uh huh," Ethan nodded.

I wrapped my hand around his shaft, pulling it closer to my lips, and gave him a gentle kiss on the tip. "Like that?"

"Oh yeah," he said.

I started to kiss up and down the shaft, letting my tongue out to cover him in wetness. "Is that making it all better?"

"Definitely," he grinned.

I moved my lips back to the top and kissed the tip again, and when I pulled back, a sticky trail of precum came with me. I let him watch as I licked the salty drip off my lips.

Leaning back in, I released more wetness before taking him in, letting it drip down the sides of his shaft. I gripped him with my right hand, using the wetness to stroke him. Each stroke was deliberate, meant to remind him of my passion. I kept the pace slow, savoring the way he squirmed beneath me, his body begging for more.

His hands clenched the floor, grabbing a handful of the rug, his knuckles white as he tried to maintain composure. His tension was palpable, but I was determined to take my time, to make this moment last as long as possible.

I kept my rhythm, thrusting him deeper into my mouth, propping him up with my hand and applying gentle pressure with each stroke. I looked up at him. I could see the struggle in his expression, the way he fought to hold back, to let me lead. It made me love him all the more.

My hands and mouth picked up the pace, and I felt him shudder beneath my touch, his body trembling with pleasure. Slowly, I slid my free hand further down, brushing against the base of his length. I tickled my fingers down to his sack and scratched my nails gently over it.

I looked up at him again. His eyes were still closed, his chest rising and falling rapidly with each breath. I continued, picking up the pace with both my mouth and hand. His back arched off the floor and then slammed back down. Faster and faster, he arched again, his legs beginning to shake from the hips.

He let out a shaky breath, his body sinking deeper onto the floor, and I knew he was about to release his tension. I could see the effort it took—the way he struggled to keep from reaching for me, to resist urging me to go faster. But he kept his arms at his side, letting me take him fully.

I focused on the head of his shaft, working faster and faster, applying more pressure with my hands.

"I'm going to come," he warned, trying to pull my head off of him.

I reached out with the hand on his sack, batting his hand away, and continued pumping.

"I'm gonna…" he gasped, cutting himself off with a loud moan.

His hot, salty load filled my mouth. I took it all in and swallowed it down, feeling its warmth slide down my throat. I stopped thrusting and pulled back but kept him in my hand. Another stream of white lava dripped from the tip, and I made eye contact with him as I leaned in and licked the creamy release into my mouth.

"Oooooh, fuck," he breathed, barely able to speak.

I swallowed the rest of him down and gulped.

"I love you," I said softly.

His chest hair glistened with sweat in the glow of the fireplace, his stomach rising and falling quickly as he caught his breath. His face was contorted in the exhaustion of his release—his brows furrowed, and his jaw clenched.

"I love you too, Molly," he managed to say between breaths.

I leaned in, pressing a kiss to his forehead before resting my head on his chest. His heart was racing beneath me, and I listened as it gradually slowed, both of us basking in the warmth and intimacy of the moment.

EIGHT

Ethan

The days following Molly's revelation were as blissful as our honeymoon. There was a renewed sense of connection between us, a deepened intimacy that colored every moment we spent together. We laughed more easily, touched more often, and shared our thoughts with a newfound openness that felt both exhilarating and reassuring. I was truly happy, but there was a shadow lingering at the edges of my mind.

Saturday evening was approaching, and with it, the ritual. The thought of meeting Elizabeth, this mysterious witch who had captured part of Molly's heart, was both intriguing and unsettling. I couldn't help but wonder what she'd be like and what this whole experience would mean for us.

We were cuddled up on the couch, the soft glow of the television flickering in the background, when I decided to broach the subject. "So, what do you need to prepare for the ritual?" I asked.

Molly looked up at me, her eyes softening with affection as she shifted closer, resting her head on my shoulder. "Mostly things I've already gathered— candles, herbs, sulfur powder, and a few tokens I use to focus the energy. I'll need to collect a few fresh ingredients from the woods the day before, but nothing too complicated."

I nodded, trying to keep my expression neutral, though my mind was racing. "And the altar? It's already set up in the woods?"

"Yeah, it's in a clearing not far from here," she explained, her voice taking on a reverent tone. "I found it a long time ago. It's almost like the place found me. The energy there is special. It's the perfect spot."

Her words only added to the swirl of emotions inside me. The idea of Molly alone in the woods, summoning an ancient, powerful witch was a little unnerving. I mean, we were talking about summoning an actual witch. I still struggled with the concept.

I took a deep breath, trying to steady my growing unease. "And... what about Elizabeth? What's she like?"

Molly's eyes softened even more, a small smile tugging at the corners of her lips. "She's captivating. There's a strength about her, but also a vulnerability. She's powerful, yes, but there's a gentleness, too. It's hard to explain. You'll understand when you meet her."

I could hear the affection in Molly's voice, the

warmth as she spoke about Elizabeth, and it made my stomach twist with a mix of jealousy and curiosity. "And what happens after she appears?"

Molly hesitated, choosing her words carefully. "We spend the night together, talking, reconnecting. It's like no time has passed since we last saw each other, but it's also like rediscovering each other all over again. It's intense."

I swallowed hard, trying to process what she was telling me. The reality of it all was sinking in, and I couldn't deny the nervousness building inside me. "And do you... have sex?"

Molly paused, looked down at the floor, and responded quietly. "Yes."

She must have sensed my unease because she reached up and cupped my cheek, her thumb brushing lightly over my skin. "Hey," she said softly, her voice full of reassurance. "I know this is a lot to take in, and I don't expect you to be completely comfortable with it right away. But I'm so grateful that you're willing to be there with me. It means more to me than you know."

I managed a small smile, leaning into her touch. "I just want to be there for you, Molly. I want to understand this part of your life, even if it's a little... intimidating."

"It's okay to be nervous," she said, her hand slipping down to rest on my chest, right over my heart. "I was, too, the first time I summoned her. But you'll see—it's not as odd as it seems."

Her words brought me comfort, but the nerves

didn't entirely fade. I think they shifted into wondering: What would Elizabeth think of me? I was about to meet a being who defied everything I understood about the world, someone who shared a part of Molly's heart.

Saturday came quickly. We spent the day perfecting the house for the trick-or-treaters—dusting, rearranging decorations, filling candy dishes, and checking the outdoor lights. The house looked like something out of a Halloween storybook, with jack-o'-lanterns flickering on the porch and eerie shadows dancing across the lawn.

"What time does trick-or-treating start again?" I asked, placing the last decoration.

"According to the newspaper, 4:30 p.m.," she said, handing me the last bag of candy. The smell of chocolate and caramel wafted up as I opened the bag and poured its contents into the bowl.

"And it ends at seven?" I asked, double-checking.

"Yep!" she replied with a grin.

"Then, we head out to the woods?"

"Yes," she said. Molly's eyes sparkled.

The hours flew by as we handed out candy to excited children dressed as ghosts, witches, and superheroes. The sound of laughter and playful screams filled the air, and for a while, it felt like any other Halloween—joyful and carefree.

But tonight would be different.

As the last of the trick-or-treaters made their way down the street, I turned to Molly. "Ready?" I asked, trying to keep my voice steady.

She nodded, excitement clear in her expression. "Let's go."

We grabbed our coats, and Molly gathered a sack filled with items she'd need for the ritual. The sun had dipped below the horizon, casting the world in deep, dusky blue as we made our way out of the house and toward the edge of the woods.

The air was crisp and cool, carrying the scent of fallen leaves and damp earth. As we entered the forest, the sounds of the neighborhood faded away, replaced by the rustling of leaves underfoot and the occasional hoot of an owl. The trees loomed tall and dark around us, their branches intertwining to form a canopy that blocked out the faint light of the stars.

The deeper we ventured, the more the atmosphere seemed to change. The air grew thicker, more charged, as if the woods themselves were alive with an ancient energy. I could smell the earthy scent of moss and the sharp tang of pine, mingling with a faint, sweet floral aroma I couldn't quite place. The ground was soft beneath our feet, the leaves cushioning each step and muffling our movements.

I stayed close to Molly, my eyes adjusting to the dim light as we followed a narrow, winding path. I considered pulling out my cell phone light, but Molly was confident in our direction.

The trees seemed older here, their trunks gnarled and twisted, their roots snaking across the forest floor like the veins of the earth. The stillness was almost palpable; every sound—the snap of a twig, the crunch of leaves—was magnified, echoing through the darkness.

After what felt like an eternity, we reached a small clearing. The moon had risen higher, casting a silvery glow over the open space. In the center stood an ancient stone altar, weathered and worn by time. A thin layer of moss covered its surface, and vines curled around its base. It was as if nature itself had claimed the space.

Molly moved with purpose, setting down her bag and carefully removing the items she'd brought. I watched as she placed candles at each corner of the altar, their wicks catching the breeze and flickering to life as she lit them one by one. The soft glow cast eerie shadows across the stones, making the clearing feel even more otherworldly.

"Can I help with anything?" I offered.

"No, but could you stand outside the circle until she arrives? I just want to make sure everything is in order," she said, placing a stone in the middle of the clearing.

The scent of the candles mixed with the earthy aroma of the forest, creating a heavy, intoxicating blend. Molly's movements were deliberate as she arranged the herbs and crystals on the altar, each item placed with care.

As she worked, the forest seemed to grow quieter, as if the trees themselves were holding their breath, waiting. I could feel the energy building, a subtle hum beneath my skin, making the hairs on my arms stand on end.

Molly turned to me, her eyes reflecting the flickering candlelight. "Are you ready?" she asked softly.

I nodded, through my pounding heart. "Yes."

She smiled and turned back to the altar. She began to chant, her voice low and melodic, the words foreign but carrying a power I could sense deep in my bones. The air around us vibrated with each word, the energy in the clearing growing stronger, more intense.

The candles burned brighter, their flames dancing as if caught in an unseen wind. The shadows they cast grew longer and darker. I watched, mesmerized, as Molly's voice grew louder, more commanding. Her hands moved gracefully through the air as she called out to Elizabeth.

Then, suddenly, the wind picked up, swirling around the clearing with a force that took my breath away. The candles flickered wildly, their flames bending and twisting as the air crackled with life. Molly's chant reached a crescendo, her voice clear and strong, echoing through the trees.

And then, as if pulled from the very fabric of the night, a figure began to materialize before the altar. The air shimmered and rippled, and a rush of cold swept through the clearing. The figure took shape, solidifying into the form of a woman. She had dark hair and deep eyes.

She stood there before us, her presence awe-inspiring. Her gaze met mine, and I felt a shiver run down my spine. This was the witch who had captured Molly's heart. I realized right then and there that this moment would change everything for the rest of our lives.

She looked to Molly, a small, knowing smile playing on her lips, then turned her gaze back to me. The weight of it all was almost too much to bear, but I forced myself to meet her eyes, to stand my ground.

Elizabeth was here.

NINE

Molly

I pulled back slightly, just enough to look into Elizabeth's eyes—those deep, endless pools of dark magic and mystery. "I want you to meet someone," I said, my voice softer now, but steady. I turned toward Ethan, who stood a few paces behind me, his expression carefully guarded, a mix of curiosity and uncertainty in his eyes.

"Elizabeth, this is Ethan," I introduced, taking his hand and squeezing it gently, offering him a reassuring smile. "My husband."

Elizabeth's gaze shifted to Ethan, and for a moment, the air between us seemed to still, the weight of the moment pressing in. Then, a warm, radiant smile spread across her face as she stepped toward him with a grace that seemed to command the space around her.

"Ethan," she greeted him, her voice soft but filled with strength. "I've waited so long to meet you.

Molly has spoken of you with such love. I'm glad she's finally brave enough to introduce us."

Ethan swallowed hard, his hand tightening around mine, but he stood his ground, his eyes locked on Elizabeth. There was a tension in his body, a hesitation, but also a quiet resolve. "I've heard a lot about you," he said, his voice steady but guarded. "It's good to finally meet you, too."

Elizabeth took a step closer, reaching out to take his free hand in both of hers. Her touch was gentle but sure, as if she was searching for a connection in that simple gesture. She gazed into his eyes, her expression open and sincere, as if she were seeing right into the heart of him.

"I'm not sure what to say," Ethan admitted, his voice low, unsure. "This is... a lot to take in."

Elizabeth nodded, a soft smile playing at the corners of her lips. "I imagine it is," she said gently. "You're remarkable, Ethan. I can see how deeply you love Molly, how you protect her, and how you give her a life filled with warmth and care. That is something I admire greatly."

Ethan blinked, clearly taken aback by her words, his posture relaxing slightly. "Thank you," he said quietly, his cheeks flushing as he struggled to process her praise. "I love her more than anything."

Elizabeth's smile widened, and she released his hand, stepping back just enough to take us both in. "And she loves you," she said, her eyes soft as they shifted between us. "I see it in her eyes, in the way she speaks of you. You've given her a happiness that I cherish, even from afar."

A tension I hadn't realized I'd been holding eased, my heart swelling with emotion. I looked at Ethan, who still seemed to be grappling with everything, and I felt a pang of concern. "Are you okay?" I asked, my voice gentle.

Ethan glanced at me, his brow furrowing for a moment as he considered the weight of the situation. "I'm trying to be," he admitted, his voice thick with honesty. "It's a lot. But… I want to understand."

Elizabeth stepped back, giving him the space he needed, her expression tender. "I want you to understand, too," she said, her voice low but steady. "This —whatever this is between Molly and me—it's not meant to take anything away from what you share. It's simply… a different kind of connection. One that's been part of her life for years."

Ethan took a deep breath, his hand tightening around mine. "So, this has been going on for six years?"

Molly nodded, her voice soft as she responded. "Since the year we met."

Ethan let out a slow exhale, running a hand through his hair. "And you love her?"

Molly nodded again, her voice quieter now. "Yes. But I never wanted to hide this from you. I've just been scared—scared of what it might mean for us. I should have told you sooner."

Ethan's gaze flickered between the two of us, the

weight of the years settling over him. "Six years," he muttered, shaking his head slightly. "I don't know how to wrap my head around it."

There was a long pause, the air thick with emotion. Finally, Ethan looked up at Elizabeth, his voice soft but firm. "I love her, you know. She's everything to me."

Elizabeth smiled, a gentle, understanding smile. "I know. And that's why I've wanted to meet you, Ethan. Because I see how much you mean to her."

He hesitated for a moment longer before nodding, his shoulders relaxing. "I don't know where this is going to go, but... I'm willing to try. For Molly. For us."

A wave of relief washed over me, and I squeezed his hand, gratitude welling up in my chest. "Thank you," I whispered.

Elizabeth stepped forward, her eyes locking onto mine, and then back to Ethan. "This night is for all of us," she said, her voice soft but firm. "It's about understanding, about connection. I want you to stay, Ethan. I want you to see and be a part of this, because you're a part of Molly's heart, and that means you're part of mine, too."

Ethan took a deep breath, his gaze steady as he looked at her. "Alright," he said, his voice filled with quiet determination. "I'll stay."

Elizabeth's smile grew, warm and radiant. She turned to me, her hands finding mine again, her touch gentle but filled with a quiet strength. "Thank you," she whispered, her voice full of quiet joy. "For sharing this night with me. For allowing me to be part of your lives."

We stood there, the three of us, the air between us heavy with unspoken words but lightened by the shared understanding that had begun to form. It was a connection that bridged the gap between worlds, between relationships, something that went beyond the ordinary.

Elizabeth's radiant smile lingered as she took both my hands in hers, her touch firm but tender. Ethan stood beside me, the tension between them softening into something more open, more honest. The night air hummed with anticipation, but there was no rush. We were moving at our own pace, letting the moment unfold naturally, slowly building the understanding we needed.

Elizabeth looked between us, her expression softening as if reading the silent agreement passing between Ethan and me. "This night," she began, her voice a quiet murmur, "is not just about me and Molly. It's about you too, Ethan. We're all here, in this moment, together."

Ethan nodded, his gaze meeting hers, and I could feel the shift in him—something unspoken, but real. He wasn't fully comfortable yet, but he was here, and that mattered more than anything.

Elizabeth stepped forward again, her fingers brushing lightly against Ethan's arm, as if testing the waters. Ethan didn't pull away. Instead, he met her touch, his breath hitching slightly but steady. They held each other's gaze for a long, lingering moment, a quiet understanding passing between them.

"I want this to be as much yours as it is ours," she whispered, her voice low, almost reverent. "No rush, no pressure. Just us. Together."

Ethan swallowed hard, his hand tightening in mine before he let it go. "I'm... I'm still processing," he admitted, his voice low. "But I'm here. I'm with you both."

Elizabeth smiled again, her gaze filled with warmth, and she stepped back, creating space but keeping the connection between us all alive. She reached for Ethan again, this time more confidently, her fingers trailing gently down his arm. He responded by stepping closer, his eyes flickering between us—between her and me.

Elizabeth's hand found his cheek, her thumb brushing over his skin in a slow, deliberate motion. "We'll take it as slow as we need to," she said softly. "There's no rush, Ethan."

He nodded, taking a deep breath as the tension between them seemed to melt away. Elizabeth looked back at me, her eyes dark and intense, and in that moment, something shifted. The air grew heavier, charged with something unspoken, something that ran deeper than the words we'd shared.

Elizabeth leaned in, her lips brushing mine softly at first, testing, tasting. I sighed into her touch, my body relaxing as she kissed me with a gentle urgency that made my heart race. The world narrowed to just the three of us—the weight of the moment sinking into every breath, every touch.

Ethan's hand found my waist, grounding me as Elizabeth deepened the kiss. My pulse quickened as the sensation of both of them so close, so intertwined with me, sent waves of heat through my body. I turned to Ethan, feeling the warmth of his gaze on me, and before I could think, I was kissing him too— his lips eager, but tentative, as if still unsure, but needing this as much as I did.

Elizabeth pressed against my back, her lips trailing along my neck, her hands sliding down my sides. We moved together, our bodies intertwined, growing more urgent, more desperate. The heat between us was almost overwhelming—a potent mix of love, desire, and something deeper that connected us in a way I couldn't quite name.

Ethan's lips found mine next, and I kissed him with a hunger that surprised even me. My hands roamed over his chest, feeling the ruggedness of his skin beneath my fingertips. Elizabeth pressed against my back, her lips trailing along my neck, her hands sliding down my sides.

We moved together, our bodies intertwined, growing more urgent, more desperate. The heat between us was almost overwhelming—a potent mix of love, desire, and something deeper that connected us in a way I couldn't quite name.

Elizabeth's hands found their way under my shirt, exploring my body. I moaned into Ethan's mouth, my body arching toward them, craving more, needing more.

Ethan's hands joined hers, their touches blending together, creating a symphony of sensation that made me feel like I was floating. The three of us moved together, our breaths mingling, our bodies pressed so close that it was impossible to tell where one ended and the other began.

In that moment, surrounded by the two people I loved most in the world, I felt a sense of completeness, of utter fulfillment. The world outside the clearing ceased to exist, and all that mattered was this connection, this love, this shared moment of pure, unadulterated passion.

Elizabeth stepped back from the embrace, her movements deliberate and graceful. In one fluid motion, she let her dress fall to the ground, the silky fabric pooling around her feet. Her body, perfectly sculpted and glowing in the soft moonlight, was like an artwork come to life. Every curve, every line of her seemed crafted by some divine hand, and she moved with an otherworldly elegance that took my breath away.

She stepped out of her dress carefully, leaving it behind as she glided toward me, her eyes never leaving mine. The magnetic pull between us was undeniable, and I felt my heart pounding in my chest, my skin tingling with anticipation as she stopped inches from me, her gaze filled with intensity.

With slow, deliberate motions, Elizabeth reached

out and brushed her fingers against the hem of my shirt. Her touch was feather-light as she began to lift the fabric, revealing inch by inch of my skin. The cool night air kissed my heated flesh, sending shivers through me. Her eyes followed the path of her hands, her lips curling into a satisfied smile as she exposed more of me.

Once my shirt was discarded, she wasted no time in finding the waistband of my pants. With practiced ease, she undid the button, her fingers brushing against my skin. Slowly, she slid the fabric down over my hips, her hands gliding along my legs as she helped me step out of them, leaving me bare before her.

Elizabeth stood once more, her hands roaming up my body, taking a moment to admire her work. The way she looked at me, as if I was something precious, made my heart swell with both lust and love. She leaned in, capturing my lips in a kiss that started soft but quickly grew more demanding. Her tongue teased mine, and her hands explored my now-exposed body with a sense of urgency.

I moaned into her mouth, responding to every touch. But even as the sensations overwhelmed me, I couldn't help but feel the tug of desire for the man standing just behind me. Ethan.

Elizabeth must have sensed it because she broke the kiss and turned her attention to Ethan, who was watching us intensely. She smiled—a slow, sultry curve of her lips—and reached out to him, beckoning him closer.

Ethan didn't hesitate. He stepped forward, his gaze shifting between the two of us. Elizabeth met him halfway, her hands sliding under his shirt as she pulled it up over his head in one fluid motion. She discarded it as easily as she had with mine, her hands already moving to his pants.

She undid the button with a flick of her fingers, her eyes locked on his as she slowly and deliberately slid the fabric down his legs. He stepped out of them, his breath catching as her hands skimmed over his thighs, teasing him just enough to make him groan with need.

Elizabeth's touch was as deliberate as it was gentle, savoring each moment as she built the excitement in both of us. Once Ethan was undressed, she stepped back, her eyes shifting between us, a look of pure satisfaction on her face.

"Perfect," she whispered, her voice like silk, before leaning in to kiss me again. This time, her hands roamed over my bare skin, exploring and teasing, while her other hand found Ethan's, guiding him closer.

Ethan pressed against my back, his chest warm and solid, his hands sliding around to rest on my hips as Elizabeth continued to kiss me, her tongue dancing with mine. The sensation of being with both of them, feeling both their hands on me, was nearly overwhelming in the most beautiful way. My knees buckled from the intensity of it all.

Elizabeth trailed kisses down my neck, nibbling gently at the sensitive skin as Ethan began kissing my back and shoulder. Their hands moved in unison—Elizabeth's fingers cupping my breasts, while Ethan's hands roamed lower, teasing the sensitive skin of my thighs.

I was lost in the sensation, my body responding to every kiss, every touch, every caress. Elizabeth's mouth found mine again, and this time, she pulled Ethan into the kiss as well, guiding his head toward mine until our lips met in a three-way kiss that was as hot as it was intimate.

Elizabeth left a trail of fire across my skin. Ethan followed her lead, his mouth finding my breast while Elizabeth's moved lower still, each kiss heightening the pleasure. My body was on fire.

"Shall we lay her down?" Elizabeth asked Ethan in a seductive whisper.

"Where?" he responded, his voice thick with desire.

They stood together, holding me between them, their movements synchronized as they carried me toward the altar. Behind the stone, the forest itself seemed to respond, and a bed began to take shape, as if conjured by the very magic of the woods. It was crafted from intertwining branches and twigs, woven together with an intricate elegance. Despite its delicate, stick-like appearance, the bed was impossibly soft when they laid me down upon it, cradling my body with a gentle embrace.

The forest had provided for us, shaping this bed from its own essence—a sanctuary woven from the earth and trees, as if it had been waiting for this very moment.

Elizabeth and Ethan stood over me, their eyes filled with desire, and I knew in that moment that what was about to happen would bind us together in ways that went beyond the physical, beyond the mundane world. This night, this love, would change everything.

And I was ready.

TEN

Any fear or trepidation I had felt melted away the instant I met Elizabeth. The moment our eyes locked, something deep within me shifted, like a puzzle piece snapping into place. It wasn't just that she was beautiful, though she was—in a way that defied description. It was the way she carried herself, how her presence filled the space around her, and the way she looked at me as if she already knew every corner of my soul.

As we laid Molly down on the bed the forest had created for us, I marveled at its delicate and perfect suitability for the moment. I could have questioned its magical appearance, but here I was, naked with a witch. Logic had already gone out the window. I felt a surge of emotion so powerful that it nearly took my breath away. I was in love with both of them, in love with the idea of sharing this night, and in love with the connection that had brought us all together.

Elizabeth turned to me, her eyes reflecting the

flickering light of the candles surrounding us. There was warmth in her gaze, a shared understanding that this night was special—not just about the physical, but about the love that connected the three of us.

I leaned down and captured Elizabeth's lips in a kiss that was both tender and full of promise. Her response was immediate, her lips soft and yielding against mine, and I could feel the same excitement, the same anticipation building within her. My hand slid up her arms, feeling the smooth, cool skin beneath my fingertips.

Molly watched us with wide, expectant eyes. A flush colored her cheeks. Her chest rose and fell with each breath. I reached out, taking her hand in mine, and she squeezed it gently. Molly's touch grounded me, reminding me that this was real—that this was happening. "I love you," I whispered.

Molly smiled up at me, her eyes shining. "I love you too, Ethan." Then she turned her gaze to Elizabeth, who was watching us with a tender smile of her own. "And I love you," Molly added, her voice filled with the same warmth and affection.

Elizabeth leaned down, pressing a soft kiss to Molly's lips, her hand resting gently on her cheek. The sight of them together filled me with a sense of peace and joy I hadn't known was possible. Every fear, every doubt, seemed to wash away.

I moved closer, my hands joining Elizabeth's as we began to explore Molly's body together. We were synchronized, each of us attuned to the other's needs and desires. The heat between us rose, Molly's body responding to every touch.

Elizabeth gently spread Molly's legs apart, exposing her wet hot center. "Look at that pussy," she said to me. "You want it, don't you?"

"Yes, I do," I said, and I did.

"Show me," Elizabeth said, a teasing edge to her voice. "Show me how much you want her pussy."

With urgency, I dove between Molly's legs, lapping at her folds. Her body retracted from me.

"Gently, Ethan," Elizabeth murmured. "I know you want her hard, but you have to treat her gently at first. Let me show you."

Elizabeth joined me, at Molly's center. She licked her thighs slowly and softly kissing her way to her center. Molly squeaked at the touch. Elizabeth stuck out her tongue, making gentle swirls up her leg toward her slit, only to veer away before reaching it. She made eye contact with me.

"You have to tease her a little," Elizabeth whispered, before returning to Molly. She licked her way back up to Molly's center, moving her mouth along Molly's folds. She found Molly's clit with her tongue. It swelled under her touch. Elizabeth moved her mouth over each side of Molly's lips, making her way to her clit with more intent. "Now you try," she said.

I mirrored Elizabeth's path up the opposite leg, swirling my tongue over Molly's folds, and then gently licking her clit with matching pressure.

"That's nice, isn't it, Molly?" Elizabeth asked.

"Oh gods, yes," Molly panted.

"How does she taste?" Elizabeth asked me.

"Like honey and vanilla bean," I replied.

Elizabeth rejoined me at Molly's center, and together we took turns lapping at her pussy, gradually increasing the intensity. Molly's gasps and moans filled the air, driving us to push her further, closer to the edge. Her body writhed beneath us, her hips bucking as she lost herself in the pleasure.

Elizabeth's hand tangled in Molly's hair as she leaned in to kiss her deeply, her tongue mirroring the motions we made below. I shifted, finding a rhythm that matched Elizabeth's perfectly. We alternated between teasing flicks and more intense strokes, Molly's moans growing louder with each moment. The taste of her, sweet and intoxicating, fueled my desire to give her everything.

Molly's body tensed as she neared her climax, her breath coming in ragged gasps. I glanced up, catching the look of pure bliss on her face, her eyes half-lidded as she surrendered to the sensation.

Elizabeth pulled back slightly, her lips brushing against Molly's skin. "Are you ready, my love? Ready to come for us?"

"Yes... oh gods, yes," Molly panted, her voice strained with the effort of holding back.

Elizabeth shot me a look, a wicked smile curving her lips. "Let's make her scream, shall we?"

Grinning, I adjusted myself and slid inside her. Elizabeth shifted, positioning herself above Molly's face, lowering her pussy onto Molly's mouth. As I began to move, Molly gasped from beneath Elizabeth.

I thrust my cock deeper. Molly's body arched beneath us, her cries growing louder and more desperate. We didn't let up, our movements more insistent, urging her toward release.

With a sharp cry, Molly's orgasm ripped through her, her body convulsing. We stayed with her, continuing our rhythmic movements as she rode out the waves of pleasure, her moans filling the night air.

Finally, when the last tremors had subsided, we both pulled back. Molly collapsed onto the bed, her chest heaving. She looked utterly spent, her skin flushed and covered in a sheen of sweat, but the smile on her face was one of pure satisfaction.

Elizabeth and I exchanged a look of shared triumph. I leaned in and pressed a soft kiss to Molly's lips, tasting Elizabeth on her mouth. "You're amazing," I whispered.

Molly opened her eyes, her face glowing with love and gratitude. "That was... incredible," she breathed, her voice barely audible.

I smiled and ran my fingers across her cheek. "And it's only the beginning, my love."

The heat between us began to rise again. I locked eyes with Molly and whispered, "Let's share her."

"Yes, please," Molly replied. Together, we maneuvered Elizabeth, spreading her legs. Molly took the lead, kissing and sucking at Elizabeth's body while Elizabeth let out a guttural almost primal moan that sent a surge of desire through me.

I positioned myself behind Molly, kissing her as she pleasured Elizabeth. My hand moved between Molly's legs, feeling the heat radiating from her.

"Can I fuck you?" I asked Molly, gently teasing her folds with my fingers.

"Yes, baby," she moaned, not stopping her attention on Elizabeth.

I slid my throbbing cock inside her. Thrusting into Molly, I locked eyes with Elizabeth, who was on the brink of her own release.

Elizabeth moaned. The sensations consuming me. With one final thrust, I filled Molly with my seed, the release sending me over the edge. I howled, the sound echoing through the woods. A moment later, Elizabeth's cries joined mine as she climaxed.

The three of us collapsed onto the bed, our bodies tangled together, our breathing heavy as we came down from the high.

ELEVEN

Molly

The forest sparkled with magic as I lay between my two loves. My head rested gently on Elizabeth's ample bosom, her heartbeat a soothing rhythm in my ear. My husband's chest supported my side, our legs intertwined in a perfect tangle of intimacy. The energy of the woods hummed softly around us, as if the very forest was alive with the aftermath of our ecstasy.

We lay in a cocoon of warmth and contentment, the world outside the clearing forgotten. Our breaths slowed as we basked in the afterglow. My body was heavy with the bliss of multiple orgasms. My skin still tingled with the memory of their touches, every kiss, every caress etched into my very soul.

"I could stay like this forever," I murmured, my voice a soft sigh as I nuzzled deeper into Elizabeth's chest, feeling the rise and fall of her breathing. "Here, in this place, with both of you."

Elizabeth's hand stroked my hair gently, her

touch as tender as the love I felt radiating from her. "The love we share, the magic between us, amplifies everything, making the world more vivid and real. Remember this feeling, this moment, every day. Both of you. Until we meet again next year."

I sighed contentedly, closing my eyes as I soaked in the warmth of their bodies pressed against mine. "I've never felt so complete, so utterly fulfilled," I whispered, my heart swelling. "You both... are everything to me."

Elizabeth kissed the top of my head. "And you, my love, are everything to us. This night was a gift, a chance for us to be together in a way that transcends the ordinary."

I nodded, feeling the truth of her words deep in my bones. But even as I reveled in the bliss of the moment, a bittersweet awareness began to creep in—a reminder that this night, as perfect as it was, would pass too quickly. The candles around us flickered softly, their flames dancing in the gentle breeze that whispered through the trees, a silent countdown to the inevitable.

"This night always moves too quickly," I said, my voice laced with the melancholy that began to settle in my chest. "I wish we could make it last forever."

Elizabeth sighed, a sound filled with sadness. "I know, my love. I wish the same. But the magic that brings me here is tied to time, to the cycles of the seasons. Once the candles burn out, I shall return back to my reality too, where I will wait another year for you."

Ethan shifted beside me, his grip on my hand tightening slightly. "It's hard to imagine you not being here," he admitted. "After tonight, I can't imagine what it'll be like without you."

Elizabeth turned her head to look at him, her eyes soft but resolute. "I feel the same, Ethan. Being with both of you is everything I could ever want, but the forces that bind me are ancient and unyielding. When the time comes, I must return, no matter how much it pains me."

A tear slipped down my cheek, and Elizabeth brushed it away with the pad of her thumb, her touch gentle. "But we have this night," she continued. "This beautiful, magical night. And it's ours to cherish and hold onto when the year feels long."

Ethan pressed his lips to my temple. "We'll make the most of it," he whispered. "Every moment, every second."

We lay there in silence for a while. The forest around us seemed to sense our quiet reflection, the rustling leaves and distant calls of nocturnal creatures providing a soothing backdrop to our thoughts. The cool night air tugged at my skin, but the shared warmth between us kept us comfortable.

"I'll carry this night with me," Elizabeth said finally, her words filled with resolve. "It will sustain me through the darkness, through the long wait until I can be with you *both* again."

I nodded, my heart aching at the thought of the time we'd have to spend apart. But I knew Elizabeth was right. This night was a gift, a moment to be savored and remembered.

The candles burned steadily, their flames gradually shrinking as the night wore on. I held onto both of them, my loves, feeling their warmth and presence, knowing this was where I belonged—here, between them, in this enchanted place. The stars twinkled above us, the forest humming with its quiet magic. And then, the candles burned out.

Elizabeth gradually dissolved into the night, her presence slipping away like a fading dream.

I rolled over, burying my face in Ethan's chest as tears began to flow. He responded by gently threading his fingers through my hair, offering what comfort he could. The pain of her departure was sharp, but this time, it felt a little more bearable because I had Ethan by my side.

Ethan, who had also fallen for the passionate and enigmatic Elizabeth, would be grappling with her absence just as much as I would. I knew he would miss her, perhaps as strongly as I did. I squeezed him tighter, and he responded in kind.

It would be our shared burden to bear, as we would both be haunted by her absence.

If you enjoyed *Haunted by Her* you might enjoy *Three of Swords* from my Tarot Fantasies series.

Heartbreak, betrayal, and a love that defies death.

· · ·

LARISSA:

I thought a tarot reading would be harmless—a fun way to spend the afternoon.

But drawing the Three of Swords turned my life upside down.

Now, I'm caught between two irresistible vampires and facing a danger I never saw coming.

Love, heartbreak, and a battle for survival...

I didn't ask for this, but I can't turn back now.

All I can do is follow my heart, even if it leads me into the darkness.

IN THE ARCANE ROOM, WHERE EVERY TAROT CARD reveals a hidden truth, Larissa faces her deepest fears and desires.

Larissa never imagined a tarot reading would change her life forever. But when the Three of Swords card emerges, it catapults her into a night filled with unexpected encounters and dangerous revelations. Drawn into the dark, seductive world of vampires, Larissa finds herself falling for Vlad, an enigmatic stranger, and Natasha, a powerful vampiress with secrets of her own.

But as ancient feuds resurface, Larissa is forced to confront the painful truths she's been running from. With hunters closing in, she must decide if she's willing to risk everything for a love that promises both salvation and heartbreak. In a world where nothing is as it seems, will she find the strength to choose love over fear?

Unveil the mysteries of the Tarot Fantasies series with *Three of Swords*, a story of passion, intrigue, and the courage to face your own darkness.

SIGN UP FOR MY NEWSLETTER AND GET A FREE BOOK today!

https://mailchi.mp/158597581671/jax-wilder

Jax Wilder

Also by Jax Wilder

CORAL COVE SERIES

Sleighed by Love

Harvesting Love

Dawning Desire

Knead You Now

Love Rewound

Perfect Lover Spell

Haunted by Her

TAROT FANTASIES SERIES: THE DEVIL'S TEMPTATIONS

Strength of the Beast

Hanged Passions

Six of Cups

Death's Embrace

Queen of Pentacles

Seven of Pentacles

Ace of Wands

Three of Swords

Two of Swords

Lovers In The Veil

Stand Alone Titles

Pride and Prejudice and Witches

Additional Books by

Rainbow Quartz Publishing

LORELAI HAMILTON

Encyclopedia of Divination

Encyclopedia of Cryptids

Tarot Tales and Magic Spells

Teenage Tarot

Arcane In Verse

The Eclectic Witch's Grimoire

Teenage Witch's Grimoire

Find Your Bliss

Tarot Reflection Journal

Tarot Refection Journal Coloring The Tarot

Dream Journal

MIRANDA LEVI: FROM A YOUTH A FOUNTAIN
DID FLOW

The Sea Withdrew

A Tear In Time

Mo(ther) Na(ture)

In Orion's Hands

Jackson Anhalt

From The 911 Files

ISLA WATTS: A FAIRY BAD DAY

Surprise! You're a Vampire

Gorgeous, Gorgeous, Gorgons

Mork The Handsome Orc

Adopted By Werewolves

Bite Me If You Can

That's The Spirit!

ROSE DAWSON'S BOOK JOURNALS: MY TIME WITH THE FAIRIES

Enchanted Escapades

Enchanted Escapades

Dewey Decimal Diaries

Siren's Songbook

Pride and Prejudice

Bibliophile's Bounty

Book of Books Journal

Pages & Passages Reading Journal

Bookworm's Companion Reading Journal & Tracker

About the Author

Jax Wilder is a passionate romance author hailing from a charming small town nestled in the picturesque Pacific Northwest. With a heart full of love and an unyielding belief in the power of happily ever afters, Jax weaves enchanting tales of love and connection that leave readers captivated.

Jax's novels are a reflection of her commitment to celebrating the magic of love, and her characters' journeys mirror the warmth and happiness she has found in her own life. Join her on the enchanting journey of love, passion, and enduring connection through her heartfelt romance novels.

www.ingramcontent.com/pod-product-compliance
Lightning Source LLC
Chambersburg PA
CBHW030503130626
46549CB00007B/2840